The Bravest Rescue Puppy©

By Dr. Gregory and Debra Bach

Illustrated by Amy Covey

To ADRIENNE
You are
Awsome

Dr. Greg Bach
Deb Bach
7-23-14

The purpose behind writing the book is to bring awareness to Lyme Disease and working service dogs.

I became a Lyme Disease research Doctor some 30 years ago when my wife who I dearly love, became partially blind and deaf due to Lyme Disease. Debra was a world famous animal trainer and had a passion for training working service dogs. Through hard work, dedication and treatment, her sight and hearing eventually returned. Two years ago my wife was struggling with severe challenges due to an auto accident.

During this time my patient Amy, an artist who was diagnosed with MS turned out having Lyme Disease and was faced with many challenges of her own. Amy needed a project to help her regain her ability to draw again so I put them both together to create this work. With great determination and dedication, we can now share this incredible true story about working service dogs, which is my wife's passion and also bring attention to Lyme Disease.

My wife says a dog should not just be chained in the back yard to be forgotten. A dog can be a companion, friend and inspiration and needs love and attention. The characters are real and the story based on a series of true events. It's to teach our children when they are given lemons not to give up, but learn to make lemonade.

No matter what challenges a puppy or person has to face in life, they too can be "The Bravest Rescue Puppy" and help save the world, even if just a small part of it.

This is Nina and her puppies. Nina is as proud as can be. She has hope that someday one of her pups will become a champion like her.

This is Lynn. Lynn and her husband,
Dr. Paul Brook, are the proud breeders
of this Rottweiler litter.

One puppy is always ready for
adventure! Her name is Zena.

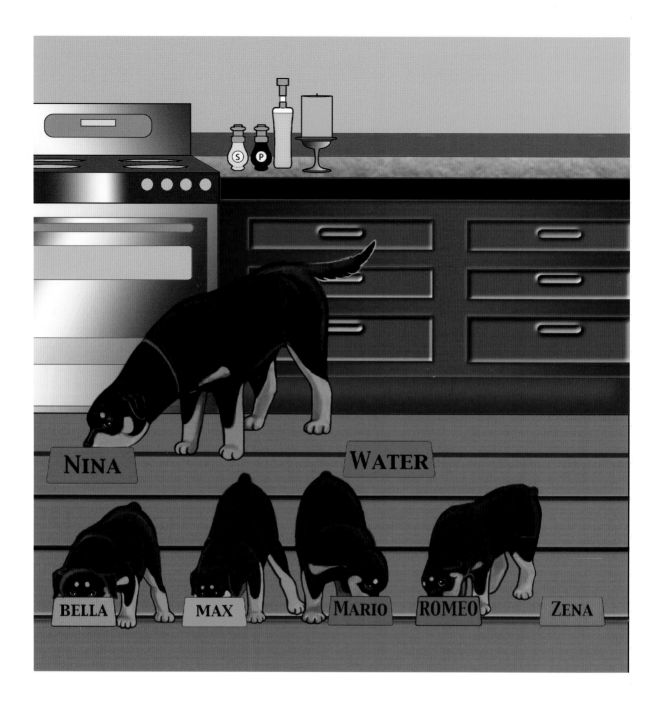

The puppies are now old enough to
eat solid food. Lynn puts food in each
puppy's bowl. All the puppies are in
the kitchen with their mother...
but where is little Zena?

Zena smells something yummy in the dining room.
She climbs on the table and helps herself to
Lynn's donut. "Stop causing trouble, Zena!" says Lynn.
Looking up from his newspaper, Dr. Paul Brook responds,
"Lynn, it's time to find these puppies new homes."

Today is a special day because people
are coming to choose a puppy to take home
with them. Watching all the people through
the window, Zena is filled with excitement.

This is Mrs. Dressler and her son, Junior.
They are looking for a female puppy to take home
with them to be their family pet. There are two
girl puppies from the litter, Bella and Zena.
Junior asks to play with Zena first.

Zena finds a fun way to play by tugging
on the loop on Junior's overalls.

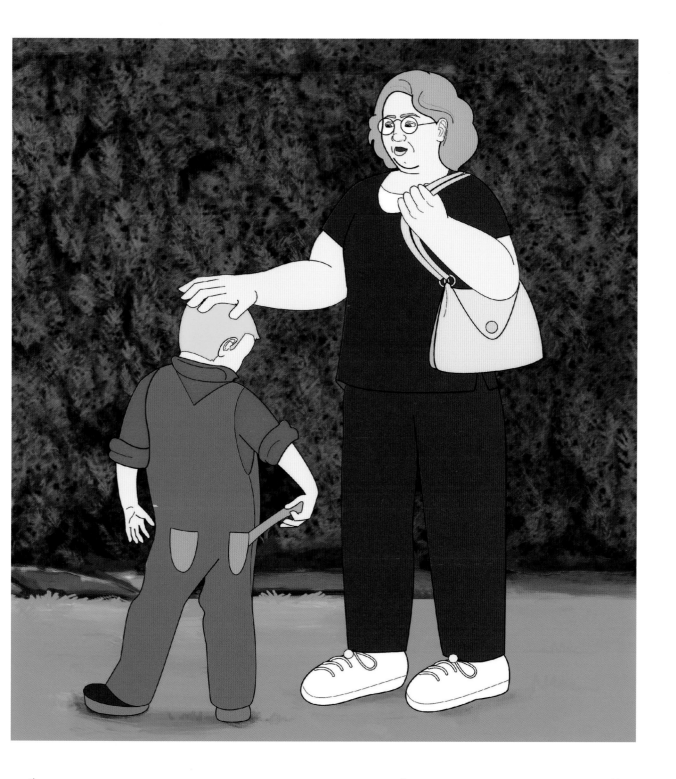

"That dog is too much trouble. She'll ruin your clothes!"
says Mrs. Dressler to her son, Junior.
"Let's look at another puppy."

Zena has more fun digging in
a potted plant.

Dr. and Mrs. Fox are here to adopt two puppies.
They look at the mess Zena made on the
patio with the potted plant and shake their heads
with disapproval. "This dog is too much trouble.
She'll ruin my beautiful plants. Let's find another
puppy that won't dig!" suggests Mrs. Fox.

Zena goes inside the house. She finds a fun
place to jump around in the living room!

Mr. Steele is looking for a puppy that won't be too
much trouble. *Look at these dirty paw prints
all over the furniture! That messy puppy is not
the dog for me! Perhaps one of the other puppies
would be better,* thinks Mr. Steele.

Dr. Fox and Mrs. Fox
pick both
Mario and Romeo.

Mr. Steele
picks Max.

Mrs. Dressler
picks Bella
for her son, Junior.

Soon all the puppies had homes.

All except one, Zena.
Why doesn't anyone pick me? thinks Zena.

Zena misses her brothers and sister,
but begins to explore the world of
nature outside.

Even inside the house, Zena is always
ready to explore, especially when she
smells something yummy.

Zena finds what smells so good and buries
her head inside a freshly-baked Chicken Pot Pie.

"Oh no! Zena has ruined the
Chicken Pot Pie I just baked!" shouts Lynn.

Lynn pulls Zena out
of the pie and wipes
her face and paws.

Then Lynn puts Zena outside to play.
"Now, don't you go getting yourself into
any more trouble," warns Lynn.

A rabbit pokes his
head out of his
burrow.

When the rabbit sees Zena, he makes a hasty
retreat to the safety of his home.

However, Zena has already
caught the scent of the rabbit.

Zena wants to get to the bottom of things.
She begins digging and pushing her way
into the rabbit's burrow.

I know the rabbit is down there,
Zena proudly thinks to herself.
I have a very good nose for smelling.

Inside the house, Dr. Paul Brook takes
a moment to think while Lynn looks out
the window at Zena.

" You know, Lynn, with Zena's energy
and playfulness, maybe she could become
a search and rescue dog!"

Lynn pulls Zena
out of the burrow.

"Leave that poor, little rabbit alone Zena!
Dr. Paul Brook is right. You could put all that energy
to better use as a rescue dog."

While Dr. Paul Brook holds Zena, Lynn calls her
sister, Renee, Lead K9 Evaluator.
Renee wants to meet Zena to see if she
could make a good search and rescue dog.

The next day, Dr. Paul Brook and Lynn take Zena to meet Renee at the training field. "Let's test Zena to see if she can do the job," suggests Renee.

"Let's see if you can climb! Up, Zena!"
Renee commands. Zena climbs up the
rubble pile to get a toy. "Good job.
What a natural climber you are!" says Renee.

When Zena is not looking, Renee hides a toy under the last cup. Right away, Zena follows her nose and finds the hidden toy. "What a good nose you have, and you're smart too! Let's go meet the other Search and Rescue puppies!" Renee says with excitement.

Renee says, "It looks like Zena is part
of the family! She would make a perfect
search and rescue dog." Renee decides to partner
Zena with search and rescue trainer, Tomilee.

The next day, Tomilee and her daughter, Maia, go to the
K9 Training Center. They see Zena training with Renee
in the distance. Tomilee waves to Renee.

Maia wants to play hide and seek with
Zena. "When Zena is not looking, I could
hide in a barrel in the rubble pile and see
if Zena can find me!" exclaims Maia.
Tomilee agrees to help Maia hide safely.

While Zena is distracted, Tomilee helps Maia
safely hide in a barrel in the rubble pile.
"Let's see if Zena can find you!" Tomilee says.

Zena follows her nose to a barrel in the
rubble. *I know there's someone in there.
I wonder how to open this?* thinks Zena.
Zena pulls with all her might and
finally the lid opens.

Zena is delighted by what she finds.
I've found a great friend! thinks Zena.
She licks Maia all over her face.
"Look, Mom! Zena found me!" giggles Maia.
"Zena could help find many missing people."

"This dog really is amazing!" says Tomilee.
"I think Zena would be a great partner
for you, Mom!" says Maia excitedly.
"This dog could do a lot of good
as a service dog!" Renee adds.

While they were talking, Maia noticed
Zena had disappeared. "Where's Zena?"
asks Maia. "Don't worry, Maia. We'll find her!"
says Tomilee. "We'll go on a search and rescue
mission of our own!" shouts Renee.

Tomilee, Maia, and Renee find Zena in Tomilee's car.
"Looks like she's ours!" says Tomilee laughing.
Maia hugs Zena with joy. "I have one gift for Zena
before she goes home with you," says Renee.

Renee comes back with a search and
rescue vest for Zena. She puts it on Zena.
Zena is proud to be in her uniform.

"See you guys in Search and Rescue
training class Monday!" says Renee.
"You bet!" says Tomilee.
Maia says, "Let's go home, Zena!"